Who But We
A Look Back From Post Apocaliptica

Lee Barmak

WHO BUT WE TO FIX THIS WORLD?

CONTENTS

What we need a is a revolution. Not an economic one, not a political one, but a psychological one. Morality is slipping. With it, the world.

"Let's thank THEM for what THEY have done. Let's thank THEM for blinding us and let's thank _our selves_ for allowing our elevated state of ignorance contribute to the blinding process."

AFTER THE THIRD WORLD WAR HUMANITY HAS ONCE AGAIN COMPLETED THE CYCLE OF BECOMING A GREAT CIVILIZATION ONLY TO FALL IN RUINS LIKE BEFORE. MOST OF THE POPULATION DIED OFF DUE TO STARVATION AND RADICAL WEATHER CHANGES BETWEEN THE YEARS 2014 – 2020. UNITED STATES, EUROPE AND ASIA HAVE FALLEN INTO A NEW DARK AGE.

IT'S STILL UNCLEAR WHO FIRED FIRST. ISRAEL? IRAN? RUSSIA? UNITED STATES? CHINA? ONCE THE NUCLEAR WEAPONS LAUNCHED MANY MORE FOLLOWED CREATING THE NEW POSTMODERN WORLD OF JOY.

CHAPTER 1

GRANDFATHER

Dear mind diary

Demonic black shadows came to me in my dream again. These horrid things flew into my grand castle and awakened me in horror. They were tall black abominations breathing death and speaking in foreign tongues. I offered all of my gold to them and pleaded on my knees so they would leave. In a demonic dark tone, they replied that they did not need my gold. I then offered my crown to them so they would leave. They replied that they did not need my crown. I then offered my country to them so they would just leave. They replied that they did not need my country. I finally gave up and offered my life to them so that I would not live amongst such monsters. For to constantly fear would not mean to live. But then, they replied. They said they came to take my inner peace. On my knees, I looked up at them and asked why? Why have you come to take my peace? They said that humanity sold itself out long ago, and it was only a matter of time before they came to strip us, use us, rape us and exploit us. Since we can do such things to ourselves then they surely can aid us in such acts.

I jumped up and awoke from the nightmare. For a moment, I did not know where I was. But, coming to my senses, I looked at myself and saw a black military uniform covering my body, a fully automatic Kalashnikov by my bed, a picture of my leader above me and others like me in similar dark riot uniforms sleeping beside on metal bunk beds.... Am I that dark demonic shadow? Am I the one who takes innocence and inner peace from kings and peasants? Why? Why do I do such things? Am I a tool who executes the evil will of others or do I myself do evil by choice? My voice is silent and yet my weapon is louder than a blow horn? Who am I?

End

"Organizingly tamed, but egotistical way of life within a system that kept most of that chaos in check on the physical plane is what life was like before the war. Screaming souls who saw this did not stand a chance. The inquisition of the material cave consumed them. In the end, it took almost no time to overpower those awakened men and women for there were few to make a difference. Out of those times came a person who is now thinking this thought... "I" ....And who is this "I"? I am but a bleep, a bleep in the existence of time, a sand of grain on a sand of grain floating somewhere in a black obis. I reflect on the uneasy past, think of the now and hope for a future. This reality is that, what I make of it. For "I", it was a bleep of uneasy bullshit."

The old man lying on his bed opened his eyes, took a deep breath and reached for his glasses resting on a small wooden stand.

"Am I happy? How can I be this happy when reality is so bitter? Sometimes I wonder, how does existence tolerate such an evil presence of humanity and its choices? Is happiness a myth? A myth hope that I hope for, a fragment of my imagination, a possible spark of light that my children have a right for? A yellow smiley face is a bullshit sticker that I always wanted at the happy age of sixteen on my car to show people that I was happy. But I have no car. I never had a car. I never will have a car. So I need no sticker. However, without a sticker, my impulsive needs subjects that, which I cannot express. A lost happiness that I could not comprehend in the first place, yet, upon my waking state I ask, where do I find individual happiness after Rome is no more and the Dark Age steals my car? Or even

the possibility of having a car?

Smiley face sticker burning and blistering over a hell like fire....”

Grandfather What depressing thoughts, was I always like this? Or is it just depressing thoughts? Am I still dreaming?

“This fanatic happy face schizophrenia lives in men now, lived in men before the war and will always live as long as the biological lungs continue to contract the molecular juice of life.

The old man paused thinking for a moment, heavily exhaling a long breath.

“Now that, I do believe is a depressing thought. It’s depressing because over greed everything rises and falls in a vicious cycle. Be it an individual, country or the world. How unfortunate for us, what a political word that is..... Unfortunate...... Depression is unfortunate, fanatical is unfortunate.....”

The old man put on his glasses and threw off the heavy blue wool blanket. Slowly sitting up he turned his body ninety degrees with his hands to sit on the side of the makeshift bed that sagged profusely in the middle.

“It’s chilly today, probably snowed the entire nigh again.”

A bright beam of early morning sun light shined through the tiny cabin window.

“How many nuclear explosions does it take to throw the weather off? I don’t know, but we sure did a good job in that department and got to the center of the pop. In one lick.”

Frost crystallized on the outside of the crude window glass during the chilly night creating unique pattern reflections on the inside. Without fully standing up the old man reached behind a wooden stand for a metal chair. He pulled it towards himself. On the back rest were his old worn out blue jeans, the kind that looked very similar to the era of Californian gold rush miners. Underneath the jeans hung a pair of plain thick gray wool socks, a white thermal top without sleeves, a thick red square patterned long sleeve button up shirt and a heavy animal fur coat. On the flat of the chair rested a pair of clean but aged yellow steel tow workman boots.

"Nothing like the feeling of stinging wool socks to wake you up."

A clearly visible uneven two inch scar on his upper right cheek by the ear seemed like it never properly healed. The thick black plastic glasses taped together in the middle with black electrical tape amplified his brown eyes.

He finished putting on the rest of the clothes and reached down under the bed, grabbing a cane that had a T shaped handle. Wrapped around the cane was a green utility belt attached to a dark leather holster containing a Colt 1911.

"The forty-five caliber atrocity that contributes itself to who I am....How emotional, that I possess such a thing. It is what it is, as I am what I am. I'm sure some famous composer had a glorious symphony as I have had mine. Short loud vibrating sounds sometimes do sound like glory. For they take another's life and protect mine. The trigger is pulled, a loud sound sings fast, and some soul involuntarily evacuates its dwelling. Nothing but cold flesh remains. But if there is no soul. Then that is truly

unwelcoming. A stoic end and nothing to worry about. "

He unwrapped the belt from the cane and placed it on the bed. As he exhaled, he leaned forward onto the cane and slowly stood up from the sagging bed.

"Let's put you back behind the stand."

The old man gently pushed the chair back behind the wooden stand and propped it up against the wall. As he did that someone knocked on the door.

Grandfather Who is it?

A cheerful young teenage boy peaked his head half way in.

Charlie Hey grandpa! Mom sent me to wake you up, the breakfast is almost ready.

Grandfather Thank you Charlie, tell your mother I will be there shortly.

The boy peaked his head back out and slammed the door. Grandfather hated when he did that.

"I need to fix that damn door."

Grandfather shrugged his shoulders after hearing the loud slam accidentally dropping his cane onto an old grey tape player that rested on the ground by the corner of the bed.

"Stuck around St.Pettersburg, when I saw it was a time for a change, Killed the czar and it's ministers."

He stopped for a second, lifted his glasses with the right hand and scratched his eye brow.

"Humm....Rolling Stones, Sympathy for the Devil. That's one of my old time favorites."

"Please to meet you, Hope you guess my name."

Sliding his glasses back on the old man turned the tape player off and picked his cane up.

"Never thought that my old ass would require a cane, a wheelchair maybe....Or perhaps one of those oxygen tanks... God damn the song is now in my head."

"Please to meet you, Hope you guess my name!"

He turned around for the gun belt and snapped it around the waist.

"Not many can say they witnessed the collapse of a civilization, the fallen angels finally succeeded and brought Babylon down to its knees..... And to think it all happened in my bleep of existence...Hell, maybe in the end it was a good thing, yes a good thing indeed, for if not for my optimism things could have been much much worse. I mean I could have died in the first nuclear explosion permanently melting my face to a wall becoming the next artsy masterpiece. Or I could have left nothing but a shadow on some metal pole. Or maybe I could have starved to death God knows where...So yes, I guess I am an optimist, or the optimist. Who would want to raise a dead twenty-first century generation of spoiled ungrateful imbeciles anyways? They were doomed one way or another. And like them I was doomed too but just so happened to doom out a bit longer."

"I shouted out who killed the Kennedy's! When in the after all it was you and me!"

"Ok old man, shut up and go eat breakfast, the most important meal of the day. No smiley face stickers, no dark ages, no bleeps of...Whatever...He who does not take up breakfast on a positive note is set to go through negativity for the rest of the day."

For some reason the old man remembered a video he once saw of Frank Sinatra telling a joke, it always made him laugh.

"Hell, when a regular person that does not drink wakes up in the morning he doesn't realize that that is the best his day is ever going to get, but a person who does drink has a lot to look forward to when he wakes up."

Slowly limping and leaning to the left side with every other step he pushed the cabin door open and stepped outside. A fresh cool mountain breeze swerved past him sending goosebumps along the back of his neck.

"Nothing like fresh air, that radiated shit down south is probably still lurking around. Beautiful day... I just hope it's as beautiful for me as it is for the power generators."

Every morning at seven sharp the breakfast was served in the family cabin. The old man had to walk only a few minutes to have himself some home cooked meals. The family cabin stood to the south, about thirty feet away from the river. Unlike grandfather's cabin, the family cabin was twice the size with two separate rooms inside. In the middle of the settlement were two turning windmill generators. Most of the time the generators were efficient enough in providing all the necessary electricity for the settlement. The windy mountain weather, all though a nuisance, was something everyone got accustomed to eventually.

Approaching the first generator, the old man placed his hand on it.

Grandfather Do me a favor and don't freeze up, a winter without power is not what I'm looking for this year.

He leaned back on the cane and continued walking towards the family cabin.

"I am a smiley face sticker that slipped through a dark crack into a time and place I never expected to find myself......I find myself somewhere where I do not know where that somewhere is.....Before everything caved in I was thinking about a possible career..... Not everything was smooth, but it was life..... The parents always nagged me to do something with my life.....Something big? Something that would have elevated my image in that foreign society of long ago....Instead I ended up building these damn generators that break down and cause nothing but problems that would discomfort even the most patient of men.... I still remember that old dream drilled inside my head to one day bring up children and grandchildren within a makeshift fake society colored brightly by Dr.Seuss books...... At one point I was even thinking that after the armed forces thing, there could have been a possible degree from a university leading to big time money, and I can't forget the small Japanese garden in the back yard with fat red koi fish in a tiny pond between the neatly stretched out sand lines of nirvana. But...... How conveniently life plans these things for us, these unexpected turns of fate, if there is such thing as fate. To walk a short distance for breakfast I need my side atrocity.......It's funny actually......Pull the trigger once and take a life. Pull the trigger twice and in the name of self-interest justification gratifies the just....The living....I'm not dead...But I am. Hell you live long

enough you get to read people's souls through their eyes. You get to know what they think before they think it. Killing, even if it's unjust becomes just. Sanity becomes insanity and insanity becomes sanity....The dreams and hopes of the old something....Something long ago....Those sweet sweet oranges, apples and reality shows.....But still that long ago be it wrong or not is not the present.....Now is now...Now is not then... We all went for the oranges without any regard for anything or anyone. With some charlatanian politics and blind faith things backlashes so hard that everything went belly up. The whole damn carnival thing from the past is still here. It was our own damn fault......We did it. Not a God or some force from outer space. We did it. We screwed up. And I am probably the last sad living monument of the past degenerate TV culture. Shit...

Charlie ran up from behind.

Charlie Grandpa! Grandpa! Come on lets go mom said to hurry up. We can't start eating if you're not there so come on.

Grandfather You little rascal if you startle me one more time today someone's goanna get waked.

"Blood will flow and we won't see, how it is, we came to be. We stumbled on to wrenched path. A dark dismay, a dark disgust. A person there, a person here. Hello my friends, the hours near."

Charlie Hey grandpa you want to hear what we learned in school yesterday?

Grandfather Well spill the beans Charlie, what did Ms. Peterson teach you this time?

Charlie We learned how you and the others survived and built the settlement, fought off the bad guys, I mean the scavengers and how hard it was in the beginning and how the elders....

Grandfather Charlie, I love your enthusiasm, but stories are stories, don't believe everything you hear. Always remember to use your head so that you can distinguish fairy tales from reality my boy. I'm sure Ms. Peterson over exaggerated a thing or two even if there is some truth to that.

Charlie But grandpa even Meghan said that the stories were true.

Grandfather Your sister like yourself has quite the imagination Charlie you know that.

Charlie But she is two whole years older than me grandpa. A whole two years.

Grandfather Making her fifteen in a few months Charlie.

"I sure did start late with the whole family thing, and to think the radiation somehow didn't get to me. So many after were born deformed, so many died young, so many still born."

Charlie Well if Ms. Peterson said it, it must be true and Meghan can back me up too grandpa so don't be saying that, you just being stubborn.

Approaching the cabin grandfather slowed his walking paste coming to a short stop. He began to feel a heaviness in his chest. Taking a few short breaths he mumbled to himself. "I hate being old."

Charlie What did you say grandpa?

"This is not a good pain...... Not good.... Shit..."

The pain in his chest slightly let go, he started moving forward again.

Grandfather Well Charlie, since you are interested in a few of those stories about the early days I just might tell you and Meghan a few of them myself if you wish.

"Hell If I don't tell you now I might not tell you ever."

Charlie You really mean that grandpa? You gonna tell me some stories and stuff? That would be so cool.

Grandfather In exchange, every day for the next week you will chop a good size bundle of wood for me and stack it on the back side of my cabin. Oh and I was thinking maybe you can sharpen the ax, sweep the cabin floor and clean up around the settlement in general.

Charlie Man grandpa you know how to ask for stuff don't ya.

Grandfather Perhaps not as good as your father, but yes I guess I can ask for stuff.

Charlie Well you got yourself a deal grandpa. You gonna tell me some real John Rambo stuff finally eh?"

Grandfather made his way up the wooden stairs of the family cabin. The red bricked chimney on the side was spewing heavy white smoke along with a strong smell of fresh burning wood. Brushing off their snow covered boots on the greenish front porch rug that read "Jackie's Auto Repair" they knocked on the door and went inside without waiting for someone to open.

"And where the hell did he hear about Rambo? Did a copy of that thing survive? The hell?"

CHAPTER 2

BREAKFAST

<u>Dear mind diary</u>

"In the hot summer months, I would sneak up behind small flies sitting on my kitchen counter and flick them very hard with my finger. Then, I would laugh at them if I saw the splattered marks on a window or the refrigerator. It's funny because now, many years into my life journey I ask myself, aren't flies living inhabitants of this place just as I? If they have even a small significant aspect how dare I inflict pain on them? But then it came to me, it's in my human nature to flick.... Just like I flick a fly with my finger something greater than myself perhaps flicks at me. I think I flicked to many flies in my younger years. I close my eyes and see the mushroom cloud. Again, again and again. Note to self. Stop flicking flies.

<u>End</u>

Bill, The old man's son in law and Mary, his daughter were moving about the cabin and setting up for breakfast.

"I am happy to see them in the mornings. It's in a moment like this that I realize all my cancerous thoughts and memories of the past stop. Even if only for a few seconds, they stop and enjoyment brought by family checks the pessimism....But only for a few seconds...
Those poor torn families of the past. That fatherless kingdom before the war. A generation of single mothers struggling to lift the poor degenerate children's souls out of the decaying money empire to a life of nothing but. Fractured families, It was so abundant."

Charlie Hey everybody we are here!

Charlie and grandfather took off their coats and placed them on the wall hooks by the window.

Mary Hi dad, how are you feeling this morning?

Grandfather Oh not bad I suppose, hey Bill how are you?.......And where is my granddaughter?

Mary Meghan is sleeping in the other room dad. She didn't feel well last night so I told her to get plenty of rest.

Grandfather Well let me know later how she is if she doesn't wake up by the time I leave. I hope it's only a small thing.

Bill tried some of the soup he was cooking up.

Bill Umm...this is actually not too bad..... Alrighty everyone have a seat now.

Bill Mary, where did you put the soup bowls?

Mary pointed to the table without answering.

Bill Well what do you know?

Mary already placed them on the table without him noticing.

Bill Ok everyone come on now this soup is hot. Charlie, place a metal trey in the middle of the table quickly now will ya?

Charlie got a small metal tray out from one of the side cabinets and placed it in the middle of the table. Bill set the soup pot right on it.

Bill Ok I don't know about the rest of you but I'm sitting down and eating this thing.

Charlie What kind of meat is in the soup today mom?

Mary Deer honey.

Charlie Man that smells good.

Mary Dad give me your plate please.

Grandfather Oh sure.

Mary poured a full portion for grandfather and handed it back to him.

Grandfather Thank you Mary.

Bill Oh yah, good stuff, Just like in a place called a restaurant eh?

"Bill you never ate at a restaurant. You wouldn't know the difference between a restaurant and a toilet."

The old man lifted his spoon out of the soup bowl with a big chunk of deer meat on it. He thought of how the rising steam looked like one of those canned soup commercials he saw on television during the late nineties.

"I remember now, this is that commercial were a burly bunch of hungry football players run into the locker room all pumped up, happy to get their hands on that "can of awesomeness" when in reality it tasted like over-preserved over-salted butchery. A picture with their athlete faces and slogans endorsed it as the holy grail of sports foods. Yes, I remember now. Preserved canned meat was just one of the wonderful pinnacles of society provided by the food industry at the time. We were a generation of morons eating commercials and their slogans. Yet, people kept on eating those commercials and spending their money on preserved waste. Pathetic....No, no, it's sad....No, I change my mind it is pathetic."

"Can you taste the awesomeness of the strength? Feed the Machine! The slogan said."

"And the funny thing was that when people made it to be fifty years of age the health problems kicked in. The fat asses, the diabetes and the heart problems just to think of a few. Oh and to fight the self-inflicted wounds the fully stocked medication cabinets were a part of a complete breakfast. Hehe, but the meds and the crap foods were actually a great balance. All in the name of convenience. Did I live in hell then? If that was hell then what the hell is it now? A double hell with a preserved red cherry on top without the convenience of meds?"

Grandfather Our hunter Danny sure is a good shot.

"How nice it would be to have some good bread right now , French bread, garlic bread...No, no, no, French bread with garlic and melted warm cheese on it....Yes that...

Charlie Soon Danny will teach me how to shoot like he does won't he dad?

Bill When you are old enough, if that is what you want he sure will. Give it some time and be patient.....You also might want to slow down and try chewing your food.

Charlie Dad, I don't want to wait till I'm sixteen dad, that's like more than forever away. I mean come on seriously.

Mary Charlie calm down, you are driving me crazy this early in the morning already....But while we are on the topic all I can say is that yes, you need to be a bit more patient. And dad, you are setting a fine example for Charlie.... Talking while eating....Let's have some civil manners while eating for crying out loud....This barbarous world is not in need of another open mouth food chewer.

"Don't forget the burping, the farting the arguing and not calling to say hello to grandmother at the retirement home."

With the taste of deer in his mouth grandfather flashed back to the killing of his first deer in the early post war winter days. Freezing wind and heavy snow fell on him and his old British Enfield rifle for hours as he lay in the cold. Finally, He pauses his breath to maintain steadiness in his hands and pulls the trigger. The animal is down, he can now eat.

Dragging the malnourished dead animal with a few others, they come up on an abandoned boarded up two story house.

"Quickly get in." One of them yells.

Prickling needle pain in the almost frost bitten hands makes it hard to cut the meat. The Zippo lighter malfunctioning made things even more intolerable, flicking the zippo roller faster and faster.....

Nothing but sparks.......No flame.....

The lighter isn't working.

One of the men taken over by hunger does not wait for the fire and bites into the cold raw flesh.

 A flame is finally lit....

The lighter worked....

The fire is going strong in the bathtub and the animal is placed over the flame.

Simmering smell of burnt flesh never smelled so good before.

Food, finally.....Nine days without it made them all crazy.

Grandfather takes the deer's head and hangs it over a fireplace in the living room.

It was a good meal....

The best meal he ever had....

Things are so funny when delusion sets in....

The bloody deer head with the broken hoofs on the white wall oozing red all over, it seemed most unorthodox.

"Barbaric. This harsh world is not in need of another open mouth food chewer in our cabin. That one fellow who chomped down on that poor animals leg in a demented rage was a sight to see…. I don't think it was even fully cooked. A deer cooked over a fire in a bathtub, I thought I saw everything at that point."

Charlie Wow mom this is good, I might get some seconds here.

Grandfather Bill, be sure to double check the generators tonight. If the wind dies down maybe light a fire around them and let them defrost a bit.

Bill Don't worry gramps ……. You built those things so stubborn all hell will freeze over before they will…….Hahahah….No worries I will check them.

Charlie Oh hey granddaddy be sure to tell me how you built the generators to, the full story and stuff. And I'm not talking about what Ms.Peterson taught us at school, I mean I want you to tell me how it all happened.

Bill I thought your grandpa already told you how he built them. Didn't you?

Grandfather Well I did but I didn't….I didn't tell Charlie and Meghan many things. Bill, I do not think I even told you everything. I just hope I have the time to do so.

Bill It sounds like someone is in for a treat, I bet you're right Charlie, even Ms. Peterson would like to hear what grandpa has to say.

Grandfather I tell you what Charles, as soon as Meghan feels better the two of you come up to my cabin, you know, the one with the door that you slam all the time...Hehehe.... And I'll tell you whatever story you want to hear. Or we can talk about anything else that you might want to talk about. Be it story or whatever interests you.

Bill Well umm gramps...just don't go overboard, I want Charles to sleep and not actually worry about the monster that crept around this place some years ago. You know that thing with big green claws and red eye's.

Grandfather Yah...... the creepy monsters, the ones that, right, the scary one.

Charlie Don't be kidding like that.

Grandfather But no Bill seriously, I think I just might tell Charlie and Meghan a few different stories that I have not told them before. He's a big boy now and he needs to know some things.

Mary What you mean dad?

Grandfather Mary....I'm an old man and I'm only getting older.... There are many things that I would like to pass on to Charlie and Meghan that I hope will help them understand our world a bit better after I am not around. I hope that now they are old enough to not just hear, but understand the things I'd like to tell them.

Bill Come on you are as healthy as a horse, you still have a ways to go. Stop talking like that. That's bad talk.

Grandfather You may be right Bill, but I want them to understand what happened and.... Why it happened. Many lessons can go unlearned and too many mistakes may be repeated. I do not want Charlie and Meghan repeating those mistakes. So I'm gonna tell them some important things this time....... And no Mary there will be no big green monsters in these stories to scare them....Hehehe.....Bill you know exactly what I mean....you lived a good deal of those lessons with me.

Charlie So grandpa, what do you mean by different stories? You still didn't answer.

Grandfather First you chop my firewood, and then I will tell you.

Charlie Oh man grandpa you still remember about that.....Well I guess.

Grandfather Charlie and I made a bargain, stories for fire wood....Hah!

Mary Oh good, just have my boy lose a finger now why don't you Dad? And for what? Some firewood? Just tell him those stories of yours without these silly demands or better have him do something else.

Bill Oh hush it will be good for him.

Mary Hey, you finish up and go check on our electrical works outside because if that thing stops turning you gonna stop turning....And I think I know what's best for Charlie ok? Take dad to make sure you don't screw up.

Grandfather Mary, I sense some animosity and sarcasm originating from where you sit, be careful you never know...You just might turn into a big green monster if ya get angry or something.

Mary Oh you shut up dad, and Bill I thought I told you to check on those darn things outside... And if you not gonna do that then you need to sit quiet like a mouse and finish you breakfast..... Oh you see what you did now? You wound me up! I'm talking to a forty three year old man as if he was a child.....And a child you are sometimes isn't he Charlie.

Grandfather Well gang this was some amazing soup once again, but I must be on my way, compliments to the chef, just easy on the salt next time. Or every time Bill is cooking.

"As a matter a fact how bout not adding any salt at all. What you trying to do Bill, preserve everyone to look good for the afterlife or something?"

Grandfather Charlie, Bill...Honey .....You all take care now...I'll probably run into you later. Tell Meghan I said hi.

Grandfather got up from the table, put on his coat and started to leave.

Grandfather Hey ill check the mills in a few myself, just do the defrost fire later...Oh and Charlie don't forget you chopping wood for me this week.

Mary Stay warm dad, I'll see you later.

 Charlie See yah grandpa.

CHAPTER 3

MATERIAL WORLD

<u>Dear mind diary</u>

"You know I can't remember who told me this, or if I read it
somewhere, maybe the bible? But here it is. If someone tells you
that God or his kingdom is to be found in the heavens, then the
birds will beat you to it, If someone tells you that God and his
kingdom is in the ocean, then the fish will beat you to it. If they
tell you that God or his kingdom is in or through a church or
temple then the holy man will beat you to it. God and his
kingdom are not somewhere out there.... But they are within us.
It is with you always, everywhere you go. So stop looking, for
you yourself are a powerful force who creates on this earth.
Create good.
Now that I think about it.... We have many good men here at the
settlement. And these men create good every day. Selfless men.
I, unlike them, was raised on television and pampered with air-
conditioning in the summer while playing shoot-em up games on
the computer.
But our men are real men.....
These men know life.
These men respect life.
They don't live for themselves.
They live for us, they live to protect the settlement, they live for
their brothers and sisters.
They live for the last remains of what is still decent on this
dammed earth.

Knowing that, gives me hope for them.
Knowing that, allows me to sleep if they do not return because
they died as good men doing the right thing.
Brave bright souls righting horseback amidst the chaotic Dark
Age forests, deserts and ruins. They patrol night and day. They
bring supplies so we can go on.
When I was twenty I was a pro at handling the TV remote. I was
also good at carrying on unnecessary false conversations with
unnecessary false friends through a web cam.
They, the few good men that we have are real men, they are not
a generation of consuming fallacies who look at internet profiles
of others hours on end and then comment on pointless statuses
of how someone just took an epic shit or ate a bomb sandwich....
These brave men are the new world war two generation that
made it off the beach.
How sad that making it off the beach is only the beginning.
How sad that making it off the beach is only the preview of what
is to come if the scavengers attack.
Oh no, I am not a religious man, not at all. I'm a fake. I'm afraid.
I'm a coward. And when I killed, I felt a void of nothing. I did not
create good. The internet age stripped me of all emotion. My
numbness and carelessness had no boundaries. Made it easier
to survive that way.
Let these good men of the now create good without the
influence of the old corrupt world.

End

Grandfather was sitting in his old chair with a stack of old magazines by his side. Charlie and Meghan sat next to the old man on the floor. It was close to sundown.

Meghan So grandpa what are you gonna tell us about today?

Charlie I think you should start at the beginning, or actually, what I want to know, is not about the war, but about how life was before the war.

Grandfather Life before the war…. Well let's see. Where should I begin?

Meghan How about telling us about what the people before the war wanted? Like what made them happy?

Grandfather That is a very complicated question to answer, but I will try.

"This could be you! What are you using your credit card rewards points for this summer?"

"Stop dreaming and take control. Yours truly Rex1000-Sport Gym."

"That red convertible is yours for only 499.99 a month with zero down!"

Grandfather I do not know if you will understand this, but before the war a significant factor that made people happy was money.

Charlie Money?

Grandfather Yes.

Charlie What is money?

Grandfather You know how we barter today right? Money was a form of barter and much more...

Charlie Ok, I know what bartering is, but what do you mean by much more?

Grandfather Slow down Charlie. First let me tell you how this money was earned.

Meghan Money was paper right?

Grandfather Yes money was paper at first and then, it became just numbers that were added to a plastic card that had all of your information. You carried this card with you everywhere and all the time. The more numbers you added to this card, the more stuff you could get and the more things you could do.

Charlie So ok, how did you add numbers to this card?

Grandfather A person had to do something like work in exchange. Some work gave more and some gave little. There was even an option to borrow imaginary numbers without working for them to get stuff if someone wanted something but did not have enough numbers.

Meghan So you had a job?

Charlie And did you borrow imaginary numbers?

Grandfather Yes and yes. I had a job and whenever I wanted something and did not have enough, I borrowed more of these imaginary numbers to get the things I wanted.

"Hey Hank what are you going to do with your first check?"
"I don't know Ray I think I'm gonna buy me some music and bad ass shoes at the store you wana come with?"
"Yeah sure, how much money you gonna spend?"
"All of it, I earned it fair and square by that hot grill so now I'm gonna spend it all."
"Oh yah ill deff go with you, I still have twenty dollars from my weekend sign twirling job."

Charlie So people worked in exchange for this money that they could not touch, then they borrowed more of it, if they wanted something.

Grandfather For many people there was a limit on how much they could borrow. Then they had to pay that money back. Also, they had to pay money for borrowing money.

Meghan What happened if you could not pay it back?

Grandfather Well, then you had to work extra hard to pay a certain minimum every month or you could end up losing the stuff you got. Then, if you couldn't pay even a minimum you became blacklisted and had to survive without borrowing. Meanwhile, the creditors made life very difficult in order to get back what you owed.

Charlie Did everyone borrow a lot of this money?

Grandfather In the end to have certain things like a house or other necessities people did borrow a lot of this money and they became trapped by their stuff. The sad thing is, that with time as people owed large sums of money, they were allowed to borrow more as long as those minimum payments were made and the borrowers agreed to pay extra for the money borrowed.

Charlie Dang, so people just wanted stuff and they couldn't get enough?

Grandfather In simplest terms Charlie, yes.

Meghan Grandpa you said you borrowed this money, how did you pay it back?

Grandfather I never did. The plan was to go to school. Back then, people who went to school had a better chance of earning more money by doing work that paid better if they had a paper that said they finished school.

Charlie You said the plan was, so you never went?

Grandfather To go to school I would have to borrow money on top of the money that I already owed. So, I joined the armed forces because they said they were going to pay for my school after four years of service.

Meghan Wait what? You had to borrow money in order to go to school? So you can make money? What kind of world did you live in grandpa?

Grandfather Oh there were plenty of opportunities for the poor to go to school for free and the rich didn't have anything to worry about. But I was part of what was known as the middle class. The middle class represented the bulk of the society. I did not have the opportunity to go to school for free. I had to pay.

Meghan Ok, ok. So let's say you borrowed money on top of the money you already owed. You went to school, and then you could make lots of money right? And pay back the money you owed?

Grandfather No.

Meghan What?

Grandfather Before the war, having an education did not guarantee someone a job that was going to pay more. And if someone did find a job, It took them a long time to pay what they owed back in the first place.

Charlie How did this money have so much power? I do not get it.

Grandfather Those people who had money could live a life of comfort. They did not have to worry about little problems. Money solved problems. But, when it came to the middle class and the poor, lack of money was a primary cause of problems. As shallow as it is to say this, people's happiness was directly related to the amount of money they had.

Charlie Was the world crazy or something?

Grandfather We lived in a money system Charlie that was a part of the everyday life. Money was power and freedom. The other sad truth is, many forgot to live life in the present. They constantly chased this money. At the time, that was what people knew and focused on. Sure there was other types of happiness to go around, but the second people could not afford their wants and needs, the world became bitter.

Meghan Did this money help after the war?

Grandfather Actually it did not, you could not eat or drink money. You could not defend yourself with money. It was worthless.

"And to think that someone said get gold. Like money, gold became worthless. A shiny metal that was worth nothing next to a clean bottle of water or a bullet."

Charlie Let's pretend that a person had so much money that he did not need any more. What then?

Grandfather Well that person would instantly become someone that other people would want to be around because a friend with money can now get you stuff or elevate your status among others.

Meghan So what you are telling us grandpa is that before the war, money equaled stuff and fame? What was this need for stuff and fame?

Grandfather What I say next may be very difficult to understand but I will say it anyways. Before the war people were very materialistic. Meaning that they had a need for things. If person A, had an expensive brand new car, he would then gain a certain power over person B, who did not have that car. Person A, could then feel good and confident about himself and know that person B, did not have what he had. The car acquired with money not only told person B that person A was able to get stuff, but he was more successful. This feeling of elevation over others gave a sort of fame and power on different levels. The explanation I just provided can be multiplied and applied to different people, different situations and many other aspects of everyday life before the war.

Charlie It sounds like person A is a jackass grandpa.

Grandfather I lived in a world full of them Charlie. I was one of them. And the funny thing is Charlie, is that If we were to go back in time and ask people if they would disagree with this, you would be surprised. No one would think of them self as a materialistic jackass, yet they would not hesitate to point the finger at someone else.

"For money they were ready to sell their mothers and fathers. Even the deeply religious put money ahead of everything when they stepped out of the churches and temples. It was all bullshit in the end. "

Meghan Was money a reason for the war?

Grandfather Absolutely. The world was walking on a red financial money line after the year 2008. Many politicians and other men of power tried to suppress the money problems. For some time it worked. But they were simply pushing back the inevitable. Then, in 2012 the world market crashed. These jackasses started finger pointing and it wasn't long after that till the war.

Charlie Did anyone try to come up with a solution of some sort?

Grandfather Oh yes Charles. Philosophers and politicians had many theoretical solutions. The problem is that it does not matter what system a country implemented. A system full of jackasses will always fail.

Meghan Meaning what grandpa?

Grandfather Meaning that greed brings out the worst in people Meghan. This greedy jackass behavior was accompanied by something called corruption.

CHAPTER 4

CORRUPTED WORLD

<u>Dear mind diary</u>

"Men are like prostitute flies in a world where self-interest is accompanied by the spider and the web. Only the human fly willingly sacrifices other flies behind it for the sake of its own benefit. The spider provides safe passage through the window for the first fly when the deal is struck. The other flies follow blindly without the knowledge of the spider . Forget communism, forget capitalism, and forget all other ideologies and systems for a moment. Human ideas for society are far from smooth if the fly willingly deals with the spider for personal gain. Dealing with the spider thus far has happened in every government, every past society, every country, every state and every city."

<u>End</u>

Charlie Corruption? What is corruption?

Grandfather Corruption Charlie is a byproducts of money. Since money gave freedom and power, people, especially those in power did dishonest things to gain more power, more money and more freedom.

Meghan Can you give us an example of corruption grandpa?

Grandfather Sure thing. Let's say that Charlie is the elder in charge, and you Meghan, decided to ask Charlie for an upcoming job opening to teach at the school since Ms.Peterson is retiring. Let's say that you really want this job and you are qualified to do this job. Also let's say that you've been helping Ms.Peterson teach for the last year.

Meghan Ok so I go to Charlie and say hey I'm gonna be the next teacher.

Grandfather Well this is where things get interesting. Jenny, who has no experience teaching, also wants the position because it does not require any physical labor of any kind what so ever.

Meghan Ok so...

Grandfather So, now Jenny goes to Charlie in private and says to him, listen, I have a deal for you. I know you want Meghan to be the next teacher, but you should appoint me instead to be the next teacher, not Meghan.

Meghan And why would Charlie give that position to her?

Grandfather So Charlie asks Jenny why should he do this. And this is what Jenny says back to Charlie. She says as long as no one knows, her father the fisherman will give Charlie extra fish every week in exchange. But no one can ever know. Charlie do you like fish?

Charlie I love fish!

Grandfather A couple of days pass and as Ms.Peterson retires, Charlie then gives the position to Jenny. He gave her the position because he made a deal with her that benefited him, even though the right thing to do for the whole community would have been to give the position to Meghan.

Meghan That is so wrong. If I am good at what I do and it helps others It should have been me.

Charlie Yes but Jenny gave me fish. You didn't. Man that is so messed up.

Grandfather Before the war, instead of fish it would have been money or some item of value in exchange for the position.

Meghan That is not fair grandpa.

Grandfather You are right. It is not fair. Before the war, we had the private sector or the corporate sector, a general political sector, an executive sector, a judicial sector and a unionized sector to name a few.

Charlie That's a bit confusing. Can you explain those a bit better grandpa?

Grandfather Sure thing. The private sector was where people tried to make money for themselves through free enterprise. I guess the easiest way to describe the private sector is if you look at some of the bartering caravans who come by and trade stuff. That system of free trade is an example of the private sector.

Meghan And how was the private sector corrupt?

Grandfather Pretend for a moment that two of the caravans that did trade with us traded lamp oil and no one but these two caravans had the lamp oil. One day, they got together and said, let's make the oil more expensive. Instead of asking two buckets of fish for a gallon, we will now ask for no less than seven buckets. Since we are the only ones who trade oil in this region and it is a necessity, we can get more stuff for it. The only thing left to do for us is to pay whatever the asking price is. We need that oil.

Charlie This does not sound like fun.

Grandfather Oh no Charlie, fun it is not. This is just a small example of private sector corruption.

"Pump that gas baby! Charge them baby! They will pay. Stupid peasants. Not like they have a choice."

Meghan The example that you gave about the teaching position, would that fit in well with the general political sector?

Grandfather You nailed it.

Charlie What would be a…. A judicial sector?

Grandfather When someone did something wrong they would be punished. The person who determined the punishment was a judge and he was a major part of the judicial sector.

Meghan The judge was like a boss.

Grandfather Sometimes a judge would punish someone a lot harder, or, not punish the person at all if the right deal was struck with the judge behind closed doors. In some parts of the world judicial corruption was much worse than in others.

"The only difference between third world and first world countries is that no one gave a shit in the third world. It was done with much discretion in the more developed countries."

Charlie Your world was ridiculous grandpa. No fair judgment, high prices for oil and the elders run the show in their own favor.

Grandfather We are not done yet Charlie. The next would be the unionized sector. This is where all the hunters, the fisherman and the scouts got together in their own little groups and constantly demanded more and more stuff or money for less and less work. At first it was a good idea because regular workers were abused and underpaid. But, with time they became so powerful that they were the ones who did the abuse. So Charlie now you get less fish because the fisherman want more days off with more pay in exchange.

Meghan In a union people got together and that was what gave them power Charlie.

Grandfather Again, the idea in the beginning was not a bad one, but as we talked about jackasses earlier, they ruin everything.

Meghan You said there was one more of something that was in trouble.

Grandfather the executive sector Meghan. As a whole, this sector, or the police as we shall call them were good people. But the power that was given to the police, was not handled properly in the end.

"More laws, more codes, more enforcement, more cameras, less power to the people."

Charlie So the police were like the enforcer who we have here right?

Grandfather Yes. The enforcers job is to make sure that peace is maintained.

Charlie They sound like good guys.

Grandfathers Any person in power Charlie naturally elevates him or herself over other people. It is the nature of the beast. In this case, the enforcers elevated themselves over the people whom they swore to protect. Then they became just like the military.

"The nuclear flash was just the beginning.

They came for the survivors.

forcing us out of our homes.

They took our weapons.

They took our food.

They questioned us, why?

Marshall law they said.

Constitution?

What's that?"

Charlie Why did the enforcers who are obviously the good guys become bad?

Grandfather Because people before the war were lost and they did many foolish things. The enforcers had problems just like the rest of us.

"They acted on orders without question. Like me, they were lost as the rest, but they had power and authority. What a dangerous combination that is…..To be lost and yet to be in a position of power…."

CHAPTER 5

A LOST WORLD

Dear mind diary

They were all innocent, all of them at birth. Then they became machines. Biological machines programmed to function within a framework of flawed parameters. This programming, this software, had problems. Many bugs. They were all innocent, all of them at birth. Then they became machines. Perfect hardware with imperfect software. And.... And that software did not just corrupt one, two or three. It corrupted billions. It was infectious. The infection grew stronger and took away the innocence earlier and earlier. Before they learned to walk, they learned of murder on television. Values? What values?

End

Charlie People before the war were lost?

Grandfather Yes Charlie. These lost people came from all walks of life. It did not matter how old they were what jobs they had or even if they were rich or poor. People were lost.

Meghan Anyone can get lost in the forest grandpa.

Grandfather What I mean is, that people were lost in their own heads.

Charlie How is that?

Grandfather It started at birth. First the young child was conditioned to live a particular way and act a certain way in order to fit in with society.

Meghan At first?

Grandfather When a child was born, he or she was exposed to a set sequence of life events that molded him or her into an adult. That adult then coped with living according to learned standards. This learned sequence of events had the right intentions behind it, but it was corrupted by other ideas and distractions.

Charlie Like what kind of distractions?

Grandfather When the child was born he was influenced to learn patterns and behaviors as I already mentioned. The problem is that before the war, the standards for values were almost nonexistent and outside distractions, or rebellious elements of life stunted the growth of virtue in humanity.

Charlie What were the values or the virtues that were lost? What happened?

Grandfather Now, before I go any further as to why people became lost and depressed and how they handled this desperation, let me tell you a bit about an important factor that slipped from the prewar society..... First of all let's look at values. Values are ideas, that are upheld to be as something of high importance. These important ideas, or, the good values, are then practiced by people to better themselves and the world.

Meghan So if good ideas got upheld then corruption would not have happened and I would have gotten the teaching position instead of Jenny.

Grandfather Yes. If Charlie gave you the position and declined Jenny's offer, he would have practiced something called Integrity. It means to be an honest person for whom things like truth and commitment to the community come first.

Charlie So a person is somehow lost when he doesn't have Integrity?

Grandfather People who lacked integrity and belief in themselves perhaps suffered the most of all Charlie. They suffered on the inside and it was pretty much every other person on the planet.

Meghan Was there a cure?

Grandfather No there was no cure, only distractions to mask over the despair.

Charlie What kind of distractions?

Grandfather Well.... People who did not have that inner light turned to temporary aids like alcohol, legal drugs, illegal drugs,

44

time wasting in front of the television and massive amounts of food. These behaviors led to only more internal confusion. Loss of hope, lack of progress and basically just following mindless patterns.

Charlie Please tell me a bit more about this integrity.

Grandfather Righteousness, honor, honesty, decency and a drive to improve. Integrity encompasses multiple values of good Charlie.

Meghan Ok, ok people lacked values. You said they turned to other things.

Grandfather People turned to things that numbed the pain of monotonous everyday life.

"The pain of self-inflicted, self-imprisonment"

Grandfather Let me get back here to where I started for now…… As the young child finished school he or she was influenced much more by outside distractions of materialistic marketing than by his teachers or parents. These young kids started to adapt to impulsive behavior reinforced by thousands of television commercials and other psychologically destructive outside influences.

"The world was for sale, peak their interest in thirty seconds and the zombie generation will follow. They were hungry for flesh. They were made that way."

Grandfather This bombardment of marketing led to the want for stuff and short attention spans. Kids could not concentrate on learning. There was even a name for it. Attention Deficit Disorder. Also, with a serving of advertisement came multiple servings of dead food.

"ADD, what a fake cluster fuck of horse shit. People came up with anything they could to point the finger in a direction away from themselves. I remember a world without abbreviations before the technological boom. Technology ruined the process of natural though. Just google that shit and get back to the video games, movies, reality shows, donuts, pizza, prozac and unicorns."

Meghan We eat dead food grandpa, nothing is wrong with dead food.

Grandfather I do not mean dead animals Meghan. I mean food that was of no nutritious value and high in sugar and chemicals. The combination of bad food and advertisement induced short attention spans made children sick and lazy. Then, many kids would mature in age and go off to higher education accompanied by ill health of psychological and physical nature.

"Dead regurgitation is what it was. Education forced down our throats in a manner of excruciating boredom. Swallow this pill of boring and learn the definitions. Why? Because you need to that's why. A dead education for a dead generation. All theory, no real world application. Professional copy and paste diplomas for all. "

Meghan It must have sucked to be sick at a young age.

Grandfather Eventually when the educational part of life was over, the child became an adult. The adult went out into the world sick physically, sick mentally, with a short attention span, with a crushing debt of money to pay back, no job and no ability to think, the internet did that. The first quarter of life experience set them up to be a struggling bunch with a loss of hope for something better. They gave up. Instead of upholding righteous principals and setting high standards, they became one with the couch on the days they did not work at a job where fake smiles went all around.

"Pity went all around. Poor little me. I can't find a job. I'm so depressed. What caused this?"

Meghan That's why people turned to drugs. They lived boring meaningless lives. And the bad leaders used that against them... Ahh what's that word Ms. Peterson taught us...

Grandfather Machiavellian....

Meghan Yes!

Grandfather One of the biggest problems actually was not illegal drugs but legal drugs. Eighty percent of the population had been on some prescribed happy pill to fight the symptoms of psychological depression. The doctors benefited more by prescribing pills and making money to fight symptoms instead of attacking the disease itself.

"But doctors could not attack the disease of depression, it was a program brought on by ill components of society that forgot its value system. A society that forgot what it was like to believe in itself. Some turned to faith and found a new strength. That was one way to get out of depression. Swap out one program for another. Uninstall complete, empty recycle bin, Please insert program for installation. Installation complete. New functions acquired. Others had kids, to live for something other than themselves. Having a child gave purpose to life again. But their diseased bodies did not produce healthy off springs. A pattern of

decaying biological reproduction of unhealthy human degradation."

Grandfather I earlier said that people before the war were lost and they did many foolish things. Do you know why that is?

Charlie No.

Grandfather When people became trapped financially, sick physically and mentally they looked for a way out. They wanted excitement, they wanted change. They wanted to feel important and alive. That was when the depressed nation backed a manipulative leader. A leader who resembled a real life superman.

"The leader gave false hopes.

Lower taxes that were not lowered.

More safety, less freedom.

The enemies are over there! Look! We must stand united as one for the fight and deal with the threat. The threat out there.

They foolishly voted for him.

Then the financial collapse happened.

And the war.

What now they said.

Doubt upon doubt.

Job hopping.

Lost, without direction more than before.

Succumbing to drugs.

Dead sex without love.

Buy these shoes, look how great they look.

Integrity? What the hell is that shit?"

Grandfather People did not have a foundation of values. Well actually they did, but it was flung into the trash bin along with the understanding of freedom and happiness. Other non-important things became important. In those final moments, the world was more divided than ever.

CHAPTER 6

A DIVIDED WORLD

Dear mind diary

The Soviet Union was a great power once. So was the United States. These two empires, as divided as they were, had something in common. Both had certain unshakable Ideas in which the people strongly believed. As different as these ideas were, they united people. People were strong and genuine in both empires because they believed in something. A sense of patriotism and belonging grasped them. Then, the Soviet Union fell apart and along with it fell the west. With the fall of the opposing empire, the control over people slips in the other.

A decline occurs when a worthy enemy is lost.

In a short time, Russia regained its strength, but when that happened, neither Russia nor the US were the same. However, they were still divided and possessed the military capabilities to destroy each other multiple times over...... Something changed on both sides. Once again the two empires clashed, but this time only militarily. The hearts and minds on both sides no longer believed. They just followed.

End

Grandfather In those final moments, the world was more divided than ever.

Meghan How so?

Grandfather The world was divided by ideas, and lines on a map Meghan. And I can explain this in very simple terms. First of all let's say that you believe in one thing and Charlie believes in another. Both you and Charlie have thousands of people following you and sharing your ideas. The problem that occurs here, is that both sides think that they are right and the opposite side is wrong. The idea could be political, religious or tied to the economy somehow.

Charlie That's cool I have thousands of people following me. Epic win.

Grandfather Because people stick to other people of similar belief, a certain mindset becomes the foundation of the region in which the people live. The region is united by a mindset. The back end of the coin is that if you have two regions with opposite views, conflicts arise.

Charlie War.

Grandfather The two bodies of people are united and yet separated at the same time.

Meghan I see how that could be dangerous.

Grandfather Towards the end, bodies of people united all over the world and at the same time grew apart.

Charlie Well I do not see anything wrong with people wanting to live their own lives as long as they do not bother other people.

Grandfather Good point Charlie. But that was not the case. As a matter a fact, this group separation, provided a major blow to all of humanity….. Things got bad. Very bad.

Meghan Well there is nothing that we can do about some things I guess.

Grandfather I have to disagree with you there Meghan. With separation comes suspicion, lack of clarity and engulfed pride that eventually leads to hate. Hate drives people to do horrible things.

"That bastard and his family said they just wanted to trade. I let them in. It was set up. They killed Kimberly. She was the world to me. I thought they were gonna kill Mary.

They thought they got me.

They were wrong.

I lost so much blood. My hip was shattered but the hate within me overshadowed the pain. I didn't just kill them, I made them pay. Hate drove me to become a monster. A monster who only lived to protect his daughter. Hate made me strong. I built walls around the camp as I also did in my mind. In Isolation hate grew stronger. The small scavenger parties thought they knew what desperation was. But desperation without hate does not make one invincible. When they lay dead in the snow I took all their shit. Their provisions, horses, weapons. Hate is a drive that makes the extermination process of all enemies painless."

Grandfather If humanity was conditioned as a whole to tolerate differences, then a mutual understanding might have been reached. Some did preach tolerance. Others wanted a one world military force.

"To preach and to want rarely gets anything accomplished."

Charlie Did you tolerate people that disagreed with you grandfather?

Grandfather I did my best. However, there came a point when it did not matter what color they were, what age, what religion, or what gender. To me, everyone was equally untrustworthy... We lost our chance. Maybe in time others can live in a world where all are free and none bring harm to others. But that's a fairytale if you ask me.

Meghan But grandfather, there must be a way for the world to exist in peace.

Grandfather The thing is, a world that is not under one flag, backed by just enforceable laws, guided by constitutional freedoms and an economic balance, will not endure. Separation will drive agendas that will cause world pain.

Charlie Are we completely lost grandpa?

Grandfather I am, but you are not. The way you think is the way you feel. The way you feel is the way you live. People's minds must be changed. But the change cannot occur by means of violence. Violence will cause fear and hate to evolve. If you do not feel an internal pull to change then the motivation for good will not last.

CHAPTER 7

SCAVENGERS

<u>Dear mind diary</u>

World peace. Right. In the end, we will stick to our tribes and fight each other. Unless the world as one finds a common enemy, perhaps a non-human entity, then there is a chance for tolerance. For we still get to express our evil nature, but this time we would do it as one big happy human family and not against each other, but with each other.

<u>End</u>

Bill opened the cabin door. He seemed distressed.

Bill Charlie, Meghan, leave now, I need to speak with your grandfather.

After the children left, Bill approached the old man.

Bill We have a problem.

Grandfather It's almost ten o'clock Bill, this better be a big problem.

Bill A scavenger party of about twenty is at the gate. They want in.

Grandfather That is not an option.

Bill Well no shit, you know though that our men are far out. We will take heavy casualties if we fight.

Grandfather They are not due back for a couple of days, I know. If the scavengers fight us, then people will die. I don't care much for them. But our people.

Bill Any suggestions?

Grandfather What is my suggestion, I guess I have a chat with them, you listen closely and after I feel em out. If they buy my bullshit they will leave.

Bill So you will just go outside the gate and make them go away.

Grandfather You make it sound easy Bill.

Bill How bout we just throw a few sticks of dynamite at them and see what happens.

Grandfather That's not a bad thought Bill. That gives me an Idea.

Grandfather continued talking to Bill. He shared a plan of action with which Bill strongly disagreed. After a few minutes of conversation, the two men came up to the main gate. Grandfather approached the scavenger waiting outside the gate by the watch tower. The scavenger was fairly well dressed in old black tactical military gear.

Lieutenant I was starting to think we would have the do this the hard way. Got tired of waiting.

Grandfather Who are you? What do you want?

Lieutenant I'm Lieutenant Hitzig. I was tasked by the new government to scout and bring in the more northern territories into the Confederacy.

Grandfather I have not heard of any government or confederacy Lieutenant. Your authority means little here. Nor have I seen any support from this government to even consider it.

Lieutenant Your men, we meet them in the south, they will not be coming back I'm afraid. They too thought like you. And I'm sorry but who is it that I'm talking to.

Grandfather I am the Elder.

Lieutenant You are the chief Indian of this place.

Grandfather What do you want?

Lieutenant Well, for starters we need to be resupplied and we need to rest. You will sign some paperwork, our flag goes up over this place and we continue on our way old man.

Grandfather From what I see, your men are tired. A fight would not be a good idea for anyone.

Lieutenant You know it's funny, my siege technician told me the same thing. But that is not relevant. We can always come back with more men. Except if we come back, the conversation of good will is likely not to be extended again.

Grandfather You said our men were killed down south. Why should we comply if that is in fact true.

Lieutenant Not all of them are dead. And they did fire first.

Grandfather I know those men, they would not fire unless it was for a good cause.

Lieutenant They were on our land and we warned them that if they did not lay their arms down they would be treated as terrorists. They were in violation of confederate code 628. Which clearly states that no arms are allowed to be in possession of non-confederate citizens or other non-confederate personnel.

Grandfather So where I stand now, is this considered confederate territory?

Lieutenant Well we must address the paper to ink as a technicality, so that you are on your path to citizenship, but other than that, yes this is confederate land now.

Grandfather Citizenship, how does that work?

Lieutenant Its cold out here, maybe we should discuss this inside. In a more formal manner.

Grandfather Sorry Lieutenant, no southern hospitality in these parts. Answer the question please.

Lieutenant Upon completion of the paperwork, this place will house ten armed confederate personnel permanently as long as it is fit to do so. You will supply provisions to the state as a tax and follow the laws of the state. Also all able bodies over the age of sixteen will serve the state for four years.

Grandfather And in return for this madness we get what?

Lieutenant In return old man you get to live and serve a greater good. You get to be a part of a new world. Enemies are vast, the confederacy is strong enough to deal with them.

"I heard this somewhere before."

Lieutenant Also it is possible that a pardon for your captured men may be expedited if you cause us no trouble here.

Grandfather You know, I have some doubts about all this. However, I think I have a solution.

Lieutenant Which is?

Grandfather I will take you to the more northern settlements and see how you deal with them. Some of them we do not get along with. If we can build a mutual trust, then we can come to terms. I need to speak to one of my advisors to make sure he approves of this if you are interested.

Lieutenant I cannot trust you old man.

Grandfather Does a word of a former Federalist Major mean anything to you? And besides you can always come back with more men. Your words.

Lieutenant The federalists are long gone. But they were men of honor. My father was killed by a federalist in the battle of Boston.

Grandfather That is unfortunate. So do we have a deal?

Lieutenant At a minimum, if you resupply us. Now, you, you do not go back in. Tell your advisor to bring out the provisions. Speak to him here, in the open. We will rest up here for a few hours and make sure we have hot food.

Grandfather signaled Bill to come outside.

Grandfather Bill, go get provisions for these men. I will take them to the next settlement by East Ridge.

Bill You are going, what do I tell Mary and the kids?

Grandfather For now tell them nothing. Don't forget to tell Maximka I said hello and make sure he is well taken care of. Tomorrow morning we will be at East Ridge. Now go.

Bill made a few trips between the men and the settlement with multiple bags of food. Grandfather sat across the lieutenant with his eyes closed. Waiting for the order to move out.

"I was never a federalist soldier.
There are no other northern settlements.
To me they could be Yankees for all I care. The name a
scavenger takes on does not make him something else.
Once a scavenger, always a scavenger. Like me."

CHAPTER 8

ON TO EAST RIDGE

<u>*Dear mind diary*</u>

Lies, Lies, Lies. The mind is in a constant state of revision. Bench pressing reality and facts becomes too heavy to lift. I cannot do it anymore. So I succumb to lies that make everything ok. A new perspective of Truth, truth, truth. When my lie is your truth, I win. You are lost and don't even know it. True victory is when I ask you for a truth and you give me a lie that I gave to you as a truth. You are so convinced. So proper. So inspired. Yet really, you are lost more than ever. It's time to eat cake.

<u>*End*</u>

The sun was about to come up. Grandfather and the Confederate men were on horseback heading north. It was a cold morning.

Lieutenant How much further old man?

Grandfather We are almost there. Maybe an hour or so.

Lieutenant I might be wrong, yet I think you are ok.

Grandfather And why is that?

Lieutenant You are willing to sacrifice other people so that your people might live.

Grandfather Is there any other way?

Lieutenant I think you will like being a part of the state.

Grandfather I've already been a part of the state.

Lieutenant The Federalists never had a state.

Grandfather Prior to the war.

Lieutenant Were you in the service?

Grandfather Briefly.

Lieutenant Tell me.

Grandfather I went through some training and then when hell broke loose and mobilization happened we were ordered to do things on behalf of the state.

Lieutenant Things like what?

Grandfather Things like rounding people up, shooting those who did not follow orders.

Lieutenant Nothing wrong with that. Not everyone deserves democracy old man. We must have rules. In today's Confederacy, you must be worthy of your citizenship. Hell if we gave it away like candy people would not know the value of it.

Grandfather How long has this institution of yours been around Lieutenant?

Lieutenant Its been twelve years in the making now. You be surprised how fast order can be restored when you have a good system. It's called not tolerating bullshit. We have most of Montana, North Dakota, Minnesota and Wisconsin under control. All in the last three years. This here Ontario territory is nice. Cold, but nice.

Grandfather Where did you get my men?

Lieutenant Grand Rapids Minnesota. And it wasn't me, I just hear of it. That's why we decided to venture north.

Grandfather Do you know how many of them might still be alive?

Lieutenant Hold on now. You shot people when they did not follow orders you said.

Grandfather Yes.

Lieutenant Is that how you became a Major with the Federalist forces? A Ruthless idealist loyal to the cause at all cost.

Grandfather No, that has nothing to do with that.

Lieutenant So when chaos broke out, shooting looters, or terrorists was not a problem for you.

Grandfather I did what I had to for as long as I could.

Lieutenant I hope then that you understand, that if you lied to me, we will come back and everyone in your settlement will be punished.

Grandfather One thing that I am not, is a liar.

Lieutenant Your men will be taken to Milwaukee and probably sentenced to the building of roads. Construction labor is in demand.

Grandfather Any news from other territories?

Lieutenant Everything south of the seventy interstate is considered dead territory. The East Coast never fully recovered. Boston and everything north of it is a fractured war zone that we are sitting out for now. The West Coast is a desolate wasteland. No one comes back from Hollywood land.

Grandfather What did you mean, when you said that citizenship must be earned.

Lieutenant Think of it, why should the state give protection to a person who could, without any contribution just come in and take. Our system requires that people give first to the state and earn their citizenship. Everyone serves the state one way or another for four years. In that time we mold loyalists. If we need men and women in a troubling time, every citizen is highly trained. The first year we welcomed everyone with open arms. That was a mistake that will not be repeated again.

Grandfather Why?

Lieutenant People must first give before they are allowed to take. If someone expects to get something without work then they will never become a citizen. They will be a no good prisoner to themselves first. Then....

Grandfather They will not contribute.

Lieutenant Correct. We will not help an injured man who is not a citizen. He made a decision not to contribute. A hard example is always made to let others know that the prewar times are long gone. Also we do not have prisons. They are a waste of time. If the crime is punishable by death, we do not hesitate considering the circumstances of the crime. If the sentence is less than death, then the guilty work. And by the way, we will give food and aid to the guilty who are working before we give anything to the lazy. We also have regional representatives in every state. Do you know why they do such a good job?

Grandfather Why?

Lieutenant For every representative we have an external accountability office to ensure that what was promised is delivered after elections. All representatives are bound to their words.

Grandfather What happens if the rep does not deliver.

Lieutenant He is exiled and forced to march towards the California territories.

Grandfather What if a disagreement arises?

Lieutenant Don't get me wrong old man we disagree all the time. That is why our representatives are very careful in their promises come pre-election time. Accountability and fear of punishment keeps them politicians at bay. As they said in the past, keeping it real.

Grandfather Interesting. How did you become a lieutenant?

Lieutenant I was young, had no direction. Enlistment seemed like a good idea. They were looking for people back then.

"There is so much truth to what he says. Desperate times call for desperate measures. But I for one do not believe that Charlie or Meghan should be indoctrinated into a citizenship. Even If I agree with it, it is wrong. In the aftermath, I was ordered to shoot a fifteen year old boy. He was merely protecting his home. His brain matter splattered all over the wall like a fly that I flicked with my finger earlier that same day. I hate my enemy, but I understand him clearly. If everything that he says is true, then the world will go on. But it will go on in pain. My tribe is a community of families. My loyalty is with them."

Grandfather So you wanted to become a part of something greater than yourself for a greater good.

Lieutenant In hell, you will make any bargain necessary to get out. I am not proud of some things that I do. But it is a must. If good comes from it, great.

Grandfather Why did you not join the Federalists?

Lieutenant Those constitution loving dogs wanted something that was gone.

Grandfather It is sad, the constitution was gone many years before the war even happened. It's a great idea. People did not care much for it. As the saying goes. Sometimes you do not know what you have until you lose it.

Lieutenant You know, you are the oldest person I have ever talked to. How did you do it? How did you survive?

Grandfather For a long time I stopped caring and did what I had to.

Lieutenant You were a scavenger weren't you?

Grandfather What's not to say that I am not one to this day.

Lieutenant Any advice then?

Grandfather Don't get comfortable. Always be ready for war. Shock your enemies to an awe so that fear grips their minds and takes them to a state of full paralysis.

Lieutenant You certainly have a bit of crazy in you old man.

CHAPTER 9

MAXIMKA SAVES THE DAY

Dear mind diary

This man who killed my wife, before I murdered him, I tied him up outside to a tree shortly after ending his brother. I then dragged his son towards him. I broke his sons legs, I did it intentionally in front of him. He said hunger drove them to do these things. He was sorry.

Hungry I said to him.

Hungry enough.......To do this?

With a small knife I cut into the boys side and ripped out the warm liver.

Here I said, holding the liver in my hand. Eat! Don't go hungry.

He did not answer me. So, instead I bit into the liver. Things started to go black. I lost too much blood.

I pulled the trigger, his soul evacuated its dwelling.

I wanted him to die in horror before I bled out. In that moment, I laughed at the broken son and the dead father. Prewar relationship irony paralleling the post war timeline in the present. Animal justice.

If not for my daughter, I would have given up then.

<u>*End*</u>

The party approached a frozen lake surrounded by tall cliffs. A light fog hovered over the ice.

Grandfather We need to cross here.

Lieutenant We will find another way old man. I'm not risking it to go over ice.

Grandfather If you go around, the horses will have to stay behind and I'm too old to go backpacking. We had conflict with East Ridge over twenty some years ago. The only reason we won, was because we did it in the winter, over ice, and by surprise. These guys will not talk if you approach the front gate. They will shoot first. Besides, after we cross we still have a few clicks to go. This her fog is good cover.

Lieutenant We need to scout out the area.

Grandfather Then you scout out the area, I'll wait right here. Better yet I'll wait for you back home if you make it back. You know lieutenant I had an impression that a man like yourself would not be afraid of a little ice. Especially thick ice that could support hundreds. You have my word as a former Federalist Major that this is the best way. I hope I wasn't wrong about you. If you fear something, then I understand.

Lieutenant Then you go first. Everyone fall in line! We are crossing the ice. Go old man, if your crippled ass doesn't fall through, we move forward.

Grandfather slowly covered some distance out on the ice and then backtracked towards the lieutenant.

Grandfather Well?

Lieutenant Everyone off your horses! Move slow.

Grandfather Lets go. I'm too old to waste time.

Lieutenant Why did you fight East Ridge?

Grandfather We had a dispute over....

Grandfather felt yesterday's constricting pain in his chest and a shortness of breath.

Lieutenant Dispute over?

Grandfather Dispute over a mine south of here.

Lieutenant Hummm...

After a few short minutes on the ice grandfather looked around and realized that they were roughly in the middle of the lake. He lifted both of his arms in the air.

Lieutenant What are you doing?

Grandfather Stretching.

The old man put his hands down and smiled at the Lieutenant.

Lieutenant What's so funny?

A small rock fell from the ridge to the right.

Grandfather Shock, awe and paralysis.

The lieutenant's eyes opened wide. He glanced back.

Lieutenant Run! Get off the ice, go now!

Before any of them had the opportunity to run, a camouflaged

Maxim machine gun over the ridge rolled out. The word Maximka was written on the side. Bill pulled the lever and unleashed a storm of bullets downward on the men. Another man standing behind Bill tossed a dynamite stick on to the ice. The explosion shattered the ice and stunned the men. Grandfather clinched the lieutenant with his arms and dove into the cold water where the ice opened up.

More explosions followed.

The lieutenant tried to swim up, but grandfathers dead weight just kept pulling him deeper into the darkness. The machine gun sound above became muffled. Silhouettes of other bodies floated motionless in the water.

"I am a bleep of existence floating somewhere in the black abyss. How did that song go again? "I see friends shaking hands, saying how do you do, when they really saying I love you. I see trees of green, and clouds of ....Forgive me universe.""

Lee Barmak

www.ingramcontent.com/pod-product-compliance
Lightning Source LLC
Chambersburg PA
CBHW071344130626
46556CB00005B/2025